Dear Parents:

Congratulations! Your child is taking the first steps on an exciting journey. The destination? Independent reading!

STEP INTO READING® will help your child get there. The program offers five steps to reading success. Each step includes fun stories and colorful art or photographs. In addition to original fiction and books with favorite characters, there are Step into Reading Non-Fiction Readers, Phonics Readers and Boxed Sets, Sticker Readers, and Comic Readers—a complete literacy program with something to interest every child.

Learning to Read, Step by Step!

Ready to Read   Preschool–Kindergarten
• big type and easy words • rhyme and rhythm • picture clues
For children who know the alphabet and are eager to begin reading.

Reading with Help   Preschool–Grade 1
• basic vocabulary • short sentences • simple stories
For children who recognize familiar words and sound out new words with help.

Reading on Your Own   Grades 1–3
• engaging characters • easy-to-follow plots • popular topics
For children who are ready to read on their own.

Reading Paragraphs   Grades 2–3
• challenging vocabulary • short paragraphs • exciting stories
For newly independent readers who read simple sentences with confidence.

Ready for Chapters   Grades 2–4
• chapters • longer paragraphs • full-color art
For children who want to take the plunge into chapter books but still like colorful pictures.

STEP INTO READING® is designed to give every child a successful reading experience. The grade levels are only guides; children will progress through the steps at their own speed, developing confidence in their reading.

Remember, a lifetime love of reading starts with a single step!

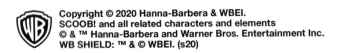
Published in the United States by Random House Children's Books, a division of Penguin Random House LLC, 1745 Broadway, New York, NY 10019, and in Canada by Penguin Random House Canada Limited, Toronto.

Step into Reading, Random House, and the Random House colophon are registered trademarks of Penguin Random House LLC.

Visit us on the Web!
StepIntoReading.com
rhcbooks.com

Educators and librarians, for a variety of teaching tools, visit us at RHTeachersLibrarians.com

ISBN 978-0-593-17872-0 (trade) — ISBN 978-0-593-17873-7 (lib. bdg.)
ISBN 978-0-593-17874-4 (ebook)

Printed in the United States of America   10 9 8 7 6 5 4 3 2 1

SCOOB!

A DOG'S BEST FRIEND

based on the feature film *SCOOB!*

adapted by Tex Huntley

story by Matt Lieberman
and Eyal Podell & Jonathon E. Stewart

screenplay by Adam Sztykiel and Jack C. Donaldson
& Derek Elliott and Matt Lieberman

based on characters created by Hanna-Barbera Productions

illustrated by Day6

Random House 🏠 New York

Shaggy is
at the beach.

He is lonely.

Time for a picnic.

Shaggy has food.

But he has no

friends to eat with.

Shaggy makes
some friends
out of sand.

They are no fun.

They cannot share

his giant sandwich.

Shaggy meets
a puppy.
The puppy is hungry!

The puppy likes
Shaggy's giant sandwich!

What is the puppy's name?
Shaggy sees a box
of Scooby Snacks.
He names the puppy
Scoob.

Shaggy and Scoob
become friends.

Shaggy gives Scoob
a special collar.

On Halloween,
Shaggy and Scoob meet
Velma, Daphne, and Fred.
They like to solve
mysteries.

The friends grow up
together.

They become a team
called Mystery Inc.

Their van is
the Mystery
Machine.

Shaggy and Scoob's adventures are just beginning!